HEROES OF INDIA: THE INDIAN ARMY STORY

TUSHAR RAJ

To the brave men and women of the Indian Army, who put their lives
on the line every day to defend our nation and protect its citizens.
Your unwavering courage and devotion to duty inspire us all, and we
are forever grateful for your service and sacrifice.

To the families of fallen soldiers, who have given the ultimate sacrifice
for their country. Your pain and loss are immeasurable, but your loved
ones will always be remembered as heroes, who gave their lives to
protect India and her people.

To the wounded warriors, who have overcome incredible odds and
continue to serve with distinction. Your strength and resilience are an
inspiration to us all, and we are proud to call you our heroes.

To the generations of soldiers who have served India with honor and
distinction, from the days of ancient India to the present. Your
contributions to our nation's history and security will never be
forgotten, and your legacy will live on forever.

And finally, to the future generations of soldiers who will continue to
defend India and her people, with the same unwavering courage and
devotion to duty that has marked the Indian Army for centuries. Your
strength and determination to protect our nation will be the
foundation of India's continued success and prosperity.

This book is dedicated to you, the heroes of the Indian Army, and to
the nation, you serve with honor and distinction.

Contents

Foreword

It is with great honor and privilege that I have been asked to write the foreword for this magnificent book, "Heroes of India: The Indian Army Story". This book tells the stories of the brave men and women of the Indian Army who have dedicated their lives to the protection of our great nation. Their unwavering courage, strength, and commitment to duty are truly awe-inspiring, and it is a privilege to be able to pay tribute to them through these pages.

The Indian Army is the backbone of our nation, and its soldiers are the guardians of our freedom and our way of life. Whether it is on the battlefield or during peacekeeping operations, these men and women are always ready to defend their country, no matter the cost. Through their bravery and selflessness, they have earned the respect and admiration of the entire nation.

"Heroes of India: The Indian Army Story" brings to life the trials and tribulations of the Indian Army and its soldiers. The author's vivid descriptions and powerful narratives will transport you to the battlefields of India, where you will experience the thrill of victory and the agony of defeat alongside our heroes. You will learn about their struggles and triumphs, and you will come to understand what it means to be a soldier in the Indian Army.

This book is a must-read for anyone who loves history, or who is interested in the Indian Army and its rich heritage. Whether you are a proud Indian, or simply a lover of great storytelling, "Heroes of India: The Indian Army Story" will leave you in awe of the bravery and dedication of the Indian Army.

In closing, I would like to express my gratitude to the author for bringing these stories to life and for giving us a glimpse into the world of the Indian Army. I have no doubt that this book will become a classic in the years to come and that it will continue to inspire future generations of Indians.
Tushar Raj

Preface

The Indian Army is one of the largest and most prestigious military forces in the world, renowned for its bravery, discipline, and unwavering commitment to the nation. In this book, "Heroes of India: The Indian Army Story," we pay tribute to the unsung heroes who have served and continue to serve, India with distinction and honor.

For centuries, the Indian Army has fought valiantly in the face of adversity, always standing strong in the face of danger and adversity. From the mountains of Kargil to the battlefields of Jammu and Kashmir, from the scorching deserts of Rajasthan to the tropical forests of the Northeast, the Indian Army has always been at the forefront of defending India's borders and preserving its sovereignty.

The tales of bravery and heroism that we recount in this book are a testament to the indomitable spirit of the Indian soldier. These stories will leave you inspired, proud, and humbled, as you come face to face with the men and women who have dedicated their lives to serving their country.

This book is not just a collection of military history, but also a celebration of the valor, determination, and selflessness that has made the Indian Army one of the finest fighting forces in the world. Through these stories, we hope to pay homage to the heroes who have given their all to defend India and its people.

We hope that this book will provide readers with a glimpse into the life and work of the Indian soldier and that it will inspire a new generation of young Indians to take up the mantle of service and sacrifice. It is our sincere hope that this book will help to foster a deeper appreciation for the sacrifices made by the Indian Army and that it will encourage all Indians to honor and support those who continue to serve our great nation.

We invite you to journey with us as we celebrate the bravery and dedication of the Indian Army. Get ready to be inspired, as you experience the thrill of victory and the agony of defeat, and to pay homage to the heroes who defend India with honor, duty, and devotion.

Acknowledgements

The creation of this book would not have been possible without the contributions of numerous individuals who have supported me throughout this journey. I would like to extend my heartfelt thanks and gratitude to the following individuals for their invaluable support and assistance:

First and foremost, I would like to thank the Indian Army for its unwavering bravery and dedication to protecting our nation. This book is a tribute to their sacrifices, and I am honored to have the opportunity to share their stories.

I am grateful to my editor, Chandan Singh, for their keen eye for detail and their unwavering commitment to ensuring that this book met the highest standards of quality and accuracy. Their guidance and support have been instrumental in the creation of this book.

I would like to thank Ankur Kumar Giri, Harshit, and Himanshu for their invaluable contributions to the research and writing of this book. Their expertise and knowledge have added depth and richness to this work, and I am grateful for their dedication and hard work.

Their contributions have added a personal touch to this work and have brought the soldiers' experiences to life.

I am thankful to my family and friends for their love and support throughout this journey. Their unwavering belief in me has been a source of inspiration and motivation, and I am eternally grateful for their love and encouragement.

Finally, I would like to thank all of the readers who have taken an interest in this book. Your support and feedback mean the world to me, and I hope that this book will serve

ACKNOWLEDGEMENTS

as a fitting tribute to the heroes of the Indian Army.
With the deepest gratitude,
Tushar Raj

Prologue

The sun rises over the mountains, casting a warm golden glow over the land, as the Indian Army stands at the ready, defending their country from all enemies. This is the story of their bravery and their sacrifices, their triumphs, and their losses. This is the story of the heroes of India.

For centuries, the Indian Army has been the backbone of our nation, safeguarding our sovereignty and protecting our citizens from harm. From the hills of Jammu and Kashmir to the deserts of Rajasthan, from the forests of central India to the coastlines of the Bay of Bengal, the Indian Army has been there, facing challenges and overcoming obstacles, always in the service of the nation.

Through their unwavering courage and relentless determination, these heroes have inspired generations of Indians to stand up for what is right and to fight for what they believe in. And yet, despite all their victories, their sacrifices often go unnoticed, their deeds untold.

It is in honor of these heroes that we present this book, a testament to their bravery and a celebration of their spirit. Here, we will recount their greatest battles, their moments of glory, and their acts of selflessness. And we will pay homage to the soldiers who have given their lives to defend India, who have faced danger with courage and uncertainty with resilience.

So come journey with us, to the battlefields of India, and discover the heroism of the Indian Army. This is their story, and it is our duty to remember it.

"We salute the soldiers who defend our nation with honor, duty, and devotion."

CHAPTER ONE

The Foundation of the Indian Army

Welcome to the first chapter of "Heroes of India: The Indian Army Story". In this chapter, we will take a step back in time and explore the origins of the Indian Army, from its earliest beginnings to its evolution into the powerful and respected force it is today.

The Indian Army has its roots in the military forces of the British East India Company, which controlled much of India during the late 17th and early 18th centuries. Over time, the company's military forces grew in size and strength, eventually becoming the primary military power in India.

However, with the Indian Rebellion of 1857, the British government took direct control of India and established the Indian Army as a separate entity, separate from the East India Company's forces. The new Indian Army was composed of both British and Indian soldiers, with the latter making up the majority of the troops.

Throughout the late 19th and early 20th centuries, the Indian Army played a vital role in consolidating British control over India, as well as in supporting the British military in various overseas conflicts. Despite the challenges of the time, the Indian Army continued to grow in strength and reputation, becoming a symbol of India's military might.

After India's independence in 1947, the Indian Army became the country's primary defense force, tasked with protecting India from external and internal threats. Throughout the years, the Indian Army has faced numerous challenges, from border wars to terrorist attacks, but it has always risen to the occasion, defending India with honor and valor.

Today, the Indian Army is a modern, well-equipped, and well-trained force, composed of over 1 million active soldiers and reservists. From the snowy peaks of the Himalayas to the scorching deserts of Rajasthan, the Indian Army is ever vigilant, ready to defend India against any threat.

So there you have it, a brief overview of the history of the Indian Army. Next, we will delve into the Indian Army's first battles, as India fought for its freedom from colonial rule. Until then, take a moment to appreciate the rich history of the Indian Army and the brave soldiers who have served in its ranks.

CHAPTER TWO

The First Battles: India's Fight for Freedom

As the sun rose over the Indian subcontinent on August 15th, 1947, India celebrated its independence from British rule. However, the birth of a new nation was not without challenges. The partition of India led to widespread violence and mass migration, and the Indian Army was called upon to restore order and protect the citizens of India.

The first battles of the Indian Army were fought in the newly formed princely states, where the rulers were uncertain about their future and the integration of their territories into the Indian Union. The Indian Army was deployed to ensure that the states acceded to India, and in the process, it encountered resistance from hostile elements and separatist movements.

One such battle was the Hyderabad Police Action, where the Indian Army was called upon to restore order in the princely state of Hyderabad, which had refused to accede to India. The Indian Army was successful in its mission, and the state of Hyderabad was integrated into the Indian Union, setting a precedent for the future integration of other princely states.

Another notable battle was the Kashmir War, where the Indian Army was deployed to defend the newly formed state of Jammu and Kashmir from the aggression of Pakistan. The Indian Army fought valiantly against overwhelming odds and was able to secure a ceasefire and ensure the territorial integrity of the state.

The First Battles of the Indian Army were a testament to the bravery and resolve of our soldiers, who were called upon to defend the nation in its hour of need. These battles laid the foundation for the Indian Army, which has since then become one of the most formidable military forces in the world.

As we look back at the First Battles of the Indian Army, we remember the soldiers who fought for our freedom and the legacy they left behind. They are the heroes who inspired generations of Indians to stand up for what is right and to fight for what they believe in. We salute their courage and their sacrifice, and we are proud of their legacy.

CHAPTER THREE

Defending the Frontiers: India's Border Wars

For many of us, the idea of a border war might seem like something out of a history book or a movie. But for the Indian Army, it is a daily reality. Along India's vast and diverse borders, our soldiers stand guard, facing challenges and overcoming obstacles, in order to protect the nation's sovereignty. In this chapter, we will delve into the history of India's border wars, exploring the challenges and triumphs of the Indian Army in this critical aspect of their duty.

One of the first border wars that India faced was the Sino-Indian War of 1962. This conflict was sparked by a dispute over the Himalayan border between India and China. The Indian Army, despite facing a much larger and better-equipped opponent, fought bravely and with determination. Although the outcome was not in India's favor, the Indian soldiers' bravery and resilience in the face of adversity have been remembered as a testament to their bravery and spirit.

Another border conflict that the Indian Army has faced is the ongoing tensions along the Line of Control (LOC) in Jammu and Kashmir. Here, our soldiers must not only defend the nation's borders but also face the added challenge of dealing with terrorism and separatist movements. Despite the dangers they face, the Indian soldiers remain vigilant, always ready to face any threat to the nation.

One of the most significant border wars in recent times was the 1999 Kargil War. This conflict was sparked by Pakistan's attempt to occupy the Indian-held heights in Kargil, along with the LOC in Jammu and Kashmir. The Indian Army, with the support of the Indian Air Force, launched a swift and decisive counter-attack, forcing the Pakistani soldiers to retreat. The bravery and determination of the Indian soldiers during this conflict were instrumental in securing the nation's borders and restoring peace in the region.

These are just a few examples of the many challenges that the Indian Army faces along the nation's borders. Despite the dangers they face, the Indian soldiers remain vigilant, always ready to face any threat to the nation. They are the defenders of the frontiers, and their courage and spirit are a testament to the strength of the Indian Army.

In conclusion, the Indian Army's role in defending the frontiers is critical to the nation's security and sovereignty. The bravery and determination of our soldiers, in the face of adversity and danger, inspires us all to stand up for what we believe in and to fight for what is right. The Indian Army may be a military force, but their spirit and devotion to the nation make them true heroes.

CHAPTER FOUR

Unsung Heroes: The Stories of India's Martyrs

India's armed forces are filled with brave soldiers who put their lives on the line every day to defend their country. But behind every soldier is a story, a story of courage, sacrifice, and love. This chapter is dedicated to those unsung heroes, the Indian soldiers who gave their lives for their country and whose names are often forgotten, but whose bravery will always be remembered.

First, we have the story of Lance Naik Hanumanthappa Koppad, who was one of the 10 soldiers who lost their lives during the 2016 avalanche in Siachen Glacier. Despite being buried under snow for six days, he was miraculously rescued and brought back to life. However, he passed away soon after due to multiple organ failures. His unwavering spirit, even in the face of death, serves as a reminder of the courage and determination of our soldiers.

Next, we have the story of Captain Tushar Mahajan, who was martyred during a counter-terrorism operation in Jammu and Kashmir. His selfless devotion to his country inspired his fellow soldiers to complete the mission successfully. His bravery will always be remembered as a shining example of the sacrifices that Indian soldiers make to protect their country.

Captain Pawan Kumar of the Parachute Regiment also deserves mention. He was martyred during a counter-insurgency operation in Jammu and Kashmir and his bravery was an inspiration to all. He fought valiantly and made the ultimate sacrifice, but his story lives on, reminding us of the sacrifices that Indian soldiers make every day to keep us safe.

These stories are just a few examples of the sacrifices made by the brave soldiers of the Indian Army. Every day, our soldiers face danger and uncertainty, but they never lose sight of their duty to their country. Their bravery and devotion will always be remembered and honored.

Let us never forget the sacrifices of these unsung heroes and let their bravery serve as a constant reminder of the sacrifices made by the Indian Army. They are our heroes, our guardians, and our protectors. We salute them, and we will always remember their sacrifices.

CHAPTER FIVE

Operation Vijay: The Kargil War

The Kargil War was a defining moment in the history of the Indian Army, a testament to their bravery and determination in the face of adversity. In the summer of 1999, India was faced with a grave threat as Pakistan-backed militants occupied key positions in the Kargil district of Jammu and Kashmir. The Indian Army was called upon to reclaim the territory, and they rose to the challenge with bravery and courage.

The Kargil War was fought on some of the harshest terrains in the world, with soldiers battling freezing temperatures and high altitudes. Despite these difficulties, the Indian Army was able to launch a successful operation, reclaiming the occupied territory and forcing the militants to retreat.

One of the key moments of the war was the capture of the peak of Tololing, which gave the Indian Army control over the strategic Drass-Kargil road. This was a major turning point in the war, and it was achieved through the courage and determination of the soldiers who fought on the front lines.

Another remarkable aspect of the Kargil War was the bravery of the Indian Air Force, which provided crucial support to the ground troops. The Indian Air Force's ability to target enemy positions with precision and accuracy was a major factor in the Indian Army's success.

Despite the challenges and hardships faced by the Indian Army, Operation Vijay was a triumph for India, demonstrating the bravery and determination of its soldiers. The Kargil War is remembered as one of the greatest moments in the history of the Indian Army, a testament to the courage and valor of the soldiers who defend India with honor, duty, and devotion.

As we look back on the Kargil War, we remember the heroes who fought on the front lines, the sacrifices they made, and the bravery they demonstrated. They are an inspiration to us all, and their story will forever be a proud chapter in the history of the Indian Army.

CHAPTER SIX

The Siachen Glacier: India's Highest Battlefield

The Siachen Glacier is a remote and inhospitable region in the northernmost part of India. At an altitude of over 20,000 feet, it is one of the harshest environments on the planet. Yet, it is here that the Indian Army has maintained a presence for decades, defending the country's territorial claims against Pakistan.

The Siachen Glacier is a unique and challenging battlefield. With temperatures that can drop to minus 60 degrees Celsius and winds that can reach up to 200 km/h, it is a test of human endurance and willpower. The soldiers who serve here must brave the elements and the altitude, facing danger and uncertainty on a daily basis.

Despite these challenges, the Indian Army has never wavered in its commitment to defend the Siachen Glacier. In 1984, India launched Operation Meghdoot, a daring and innovative military operation that secured the glacier and prevented Pakistan from advancing into the region. Since then, the Indian Army has maintained a continuous presence on the glacier, braving the elements and the hostile terrain to protect their country.

The soldiers who serve on the Siachen Glacier are truly the epitome of courage and determination. They live in austere conditions, relying on a tenuous supply line for their food, water, and other necessities. They face constant danger from avalanches, frostbite, and other environmental hazards, but they never lose sight of their duty to their country.

For years, the Siachen Glacier has been a symbol of the Indian Army's bravery and commitment to defending their country. It is a testament to the resilience and determination of our soldiers, who stand guard over this inhospitable terrain, facing danger and uncertainty, but never losing sight of their duty to India.

In conclusion, the Siachen Glacier is a remarkable and inspiring story of the Indian Army. It is a testament to the bravery and determination of our soldiers, who stand guard over this inhospitable terrain, facing danger and uncertainty, but never losing sight of their duty to India. The Siachen Glacier is a symbol of India's strength and resilience, and it is a reminder of the sacrifices that our soldiers make to defend our country.

CHAPTER SEVEN

The Indian Peacekeeping Force: Upholding Peace in Crisis Zones

The Indian Peacekeeping Force, or IPKF, is a crucial component of the Indian Army and a testament to India's commitment to maintaining peace and stability in crisis-ridden regions around the world. Formed in 1948, the IPKF has played a significant role in promoting peace and resolving conflicts in countries such as Sri Lanka, East Timor, and the Democratic Republic of Congo.

The IPKF operates under the umbrella of the United Nations and is responsible for carrying out peacekeeping operations in conflict-torn regions. Its tasks include maintaining peace and security, monitoring ceasefire agreements, protecting civilians, and assisting in the reconstruction of war-torn countries. The IPKF is also tasked with assisting in the implementation of the political process and promoting the rule of law.

The IPKF operates in some of the most dangerous and challenging environments in the world, and its soldiers are trained to handle complex and volatile situations. They are equipped with the latest technology and weapons, but their most important weapon is their training and experience in handling such situations. Their courage and resilience in the face of danger have earned them the respect and admiration of the people they serve.

One of the most significant peacekeeping missions undertaken by the IPKF was in Sri Lanka, where it was deployed to restore peace in the country after a civil war broke out. The IPKF played a key role in maintaining peace and stability, and its soldiers worked tirelessly to ensure that civilians were protected and the peace process was successful.

The Indian Peacekeeping Force is a symbol of India's commitment to promoting peace and stability in the world. Its soldiers are true heroes who put their lives on the line to ensure that others can live in peace. Whether they are patrolling the streets of a war-torn city or helping to rebuild a devastated country, the IPKF always operates with the goal of promoting peace and stability in the world.

In conclusion, the Indian Peacekeeping Force is a crucial component of the Indian Army and a testament to India's commitment to peace and stability. Its soldiers are heroes who put their lives on the line to ensure that others can live in peace, and their courage and resilience will always be remembered and celebrated.

CHAPTER EIGHT

The Special Forces: India's Elite Warriors

Welcome to the world of India's elite warriors, the Special Forces. These brave soldiers are some of the most highly trained and skilled warriors in the Indian Army, and they are the front line of defense when it comes to the most dangerous and complex missions.

The Special Forces are responsible for conducting a wide range of operations, from unconventional warfare to counter-terrorism, and their skills and abilities are unmatched. These soldiers undergo extensive training and are equipped with the latest technology and weapons to carry out their missions with precision and accuracy.

One of the most well-known units in the Special Forces is the Para Commandos, a unit that has been instrumental in many of India's most important military operations. The Para Commandos are known for their quick response time, their ability to operate in hostile environments, and their relentless pursuit of their objectives.

Another important unit in the Special Forces is the Garud Commando Force, which is responsible for a wide range of tasks, including reconnaissance, direct action, and special reconnaissance. The Garud Commandos are known for their bravery and their unwavering determination, and they are highly respected by their fellow soldiers and the people of India.

So, what sets the Special Forces apart from the rest of the Indian Army? Well, it's their intense training and their unwavering commitment to their mission. These soldiers undergo a rigorous selection process, which tests their physical and mental abilities, as well as their courage and resolves. Only the most elite soldiers are selected to join the Special Forces, and their training is unlike anything you've ever seen.

From survival training in remote and inhospitable environments to weapons and combat training, the Special Forces are equipped with the skills and knowledge they need to succeed in any situation. And their commitment to their mission is unrivaled. These soldiers are willing to put their lives on the line to defend their country, and they do so with pride and honor.

In conclusion, the Special Forces are the elite warriors of the Indian Army, and their bravery and skill are unmatched. These soldiers are the first line of defense in India's most dangerous missions, and their commitment to their country and their fellow soldiers is truly inspiring. So, the next time you hear about the Special Forces, remember these brave soldiers who put their lives on the line every day to defend India.

CHAPTER NINE

Operation Parakram: India's Response to Terrorism

In the world we live in today, terrorism is a threat that looms large over every nation. India is no exception, and the country has seen its fair share of terrorist attacks over the years. But when the nation is faced with such a threat, the Indian Army is always ready to respond. One such response was Operation Parakram, a military operation that was launched in response to a series of terrorist attacks on Indian soil.

Operation Parakram was launched in December 2001, after terrorists attacked the Indian Parliament in New Delhi. The operation was designed to send a clear message to the world that India would not tolerate terrorism in any form and that the country was prepared to take strong action against those who threatened its security.

Under the leadership of the then-Chief of Army Staff, General S. Padmanabhan, the Indian Army was mobilized, and troops were deployed along the border with Pakistan. The operation involved a massive mobilization of troops, and the Indian Army was prepared to take on any threat that might come it's way.

Despite the scale of the operation, the Indian Army showed remarkable restraint, and the situation was defused without any major conflict. The troops remained deployed along the border for a number of months, and the operation was eventually called off after the two sides reached an understanding.

What made Operation Parakram so significant was that it showed the world that India was prepared to stand up for itself and that the country would not be intimidated by terrorism. The Indian Army's readiness and commitment to the mission was a testament to the bravery and skill of its soldiers, and it demonstrated to the world that India was a force to be reckoned with.

In conclusion, Operation Parakram was a defining moment in the history of the Indian Army, and it showed the world that India was ready and willing to take on the threat of terrorism. The bravery and commitment of the Indian Army in the face of such a threat were truly inspiring, and it is a reminder that the Indian Army is always ready to defend the nation and its citizens. So, let us remember the soldiers who served in Operation Parakram, and let us honor their bravery and their commitment to the nation.

CHAPTER TEN

The Humanitarian Missions: India's Helping Hand in Disasters

The Indian Army is not just a fighting force, it's also a force for good. And this is never more evident than during times of natural disasters and humanitarian crises when the Indian Army is called upon to lend a helping hand.

From earthquakes to floods, the Indian Army is always ready to lend its support, providing aid, relief, and comfort to those in need. Their quick response time and their ability to operate in difficult environments make them valuable assets in times of crisis, and their dedication and compassion are an inspiration to all.

One of the most well-known humanitarian missions carried out by the Indian Army was during the 2004 Indian Ocean tsunami. The Indian Army was among the first responders, providing aid, relief, and comfort to the survivors of this devastating disaster. They worked tirelessly to rescue those in need, provide food and shelter, and help rebuild the communities that had been destroyed.

Another notable omission was the relief efforts during the 2013 Uttarakhand floods. The Indian Army was instrumental in rescuing those who were trapped and providing aid to the survivors. Their quick response time and their ability to operate in difficult terrain made all the difference, and their unwavering commitment to helping others was truly inspiring.

It's not just in India that the Indian Army lends a helping hand. They have also been instrumental in providing aid and relief during natural disasters in other countries, including Nepal and Bangladesh. Their compassion and their willingness to help others, no matter where they are, is a testament to the values and principles of the Indian Army.

So, why is the Indian Army's role in humanitarian missions so important? Well, it's simple. They provide hope and comfort to those in need, and they show that even in the darkest of times, there is always someone there to help. Their compassion and their dedication to helping others are truly inspiring, and it's a reminders of the best of what humanity can achieve.

In conclusion, the Indian Army's role in humanitarian missions is a testament to its commitment to helping others, no matter the circumstances. Their bravery and their compassion are an inspiration to all, and their unwavering dedication to their mission is a shining example of what it means to be a hero. So, the next time you hear about the Indian Army's efforts in a humanitarian crisis, remember these brave soldiers who put the needs of others before their own.

CHAPTER ELEVEN

The Women Warriors: India's Female Soldiers

Welcome to the world of India's female soldiers, the women warriors who have broken down barriers and paved the way for other women in the Indian Army. These brave women have shown that gender should never be a barrier to serving their country and that their dedication and bravery are just as strong as their male counterparts.

Women have been serving in the Indian Army since the late 1940s, and they have come a long way since then. Today, women are playing a crucial role in all aspects of the Indian Army, from combat to peacekeeping, and their contributions are immeasurable.

One of the most well-known units for female soldiers is the Corps of Military Police, which is responsible for maintaining law and order, as well as investigating crimes within the Indian Army. The women in this unit are trained in a wide range of skills, from weapons training to criminal investigation, and they are instrumental in ensuring that the Indian Army operates with the highest standards of discipline and professionalism.

Another important unit for female soldiers is the Army Medical Corps, which is responsible for providing medical care to the soldiers of the Indian Army. These women are trained in a wide range of medical skills, from surgery to nursing, and they play a critical role in keeping the soldiers of the Indian Army healthy and fit.

So, what sets the women warriors of the Indian Army apart from the rest of the women in India? Well, it's their courage and their unwavering dedication to their country. These women have chosen to serve their country, and they do so with pride and honor. They undergo the same rigorous training as their male counterparts, and they are equipped with the skills and knowledge they need to succeed in any situation.

And their impact on the Indian Army is immeasurable. They have shown that women are just as capable as men when it comes to serving their country, and they have inspired other women to follow in their footsteps. These women warriors have shown that women can be strong, brave, and dedicated and that they are more than capable of playing a critical role in the Indian Army.

In conclusion, the women warriors of the Indian Army are trailblazers and role models for women all across India. They have proven that women can be just as brave and dedicated as men, and their contributions to the Indian Army are immeasurable. So, the next time you hear about the women warriors of the Indian Army, remember these brave women who have shown that anything is possible.

CHAPTER TWELVE

The Legacy of the Indian Army: The Future of India's Defense Force.

The Indian Army has a rich and proud history, one that is filled with bravery, sacrifice, and honor. And as we look to the future, we can be confident that the legacy of the Indian Army will continue to inspire generations to come.

In the past, the Indian Army has faced many challenges, from defending India's borders to responding to natural disasters and terrorist attacks. And in every situation, the soldiers of the Indian Army have risen to the occasion, exhibiting the courage and determination that has become synonymous with India's defense force.

As we look to the future, we can expect the Indian Army to continue to play a critical role in maintaining peace and security in India and around the world. The challenges facing India are numerous, from threats of terrorism to the changing geopolitical landscape, but the Indian Army is ready and capable of meeting these challenges head-on.

To ensure that the Indian Army is prepared for the future, the government and military leaders have made significant investments in modernizing the force. This includes acquiring new weapons and technology, improving training and education programs, and enhancing the overall readiness of the Indian Army.

In addition to these investments, the Indian Army is also focused on promoting diversity and inclusiveness within its ranks. This includes increasing the number of women in the military, as well as ensuring that soldiers from all regions and backgrounds have equal opportunities to serve and succeed.

In conclusion, the Indian Army is a national treasure, one that has served India with distinction for centuries. And as we look to the future, we can be confident that the legacy of the Indian Army will continue to inspire generations of Indians to stand up for what is right and to defend their country with bravery and honor. So, let us continue to celebrate the achievements of the Indian Army, and let us always remember the sacrifices of our brave soldiers who have given their lives to defend India.

* 9 7 9 8 8 8 9 5 9 5 1 7 5 *